Kitty, Kitty, Come Find Me!

Rose Leclair

AuthorHouse™
1663 Liberty Drive
Bloomington, IN 47403
www.authorhouse.com
Phone: 1 (800) 839-8640

Published by AuthorHouse 09/07/2018

Library of Congress Control Number: 2018910620

ISBN: 978-1-5462-5903-9 (sc)
ISBN: 978-1-5462-5902-2 (e)

Print information available on the last page.

This book is printed on acid-free paper.

authorHOUSE®

Kitty, Kitty, Come Find Me!

Kitty, Kitty, come find me!

I'm hiding on a branch
of a Hickory Tree!

Kitty, Kitty, come find me!

I'm hiding in a log near the deep blue sea!

Kitty, Kitty, come find me!

I'm hiding on the home of a honeybee!

Kitty, Kitty, come find me!

I'm sitting on the petal
of a Tiger Lily!

Kitty, Kitty, come find me!

I'm sitting on top
of a blueberry!

Kitty, Kitty, come and see!

It's time to rest for you and me!

Printed in the United States
By Bookmasters